DINOSAUR DIG

DINOSAUR DIG

BY Kathryn Lasky · PHOTOGRAPHS BY Christopher G. Knight

MORROW JUNIOR BOOKS · NEW YORK

We would like to thank Keith Rigby, Jr., for taking us along on a marvelous adventure and for his continued support of this project. Dr. Rigby's excavations in Montana are partially supported by Earthwatch, a nonprofit organization that supports various scientific expeditions around the world.

We are also grateful to our friend, Jeanne Hanson, for her energy and enthusiasm in making arrangements for our families to participate in Keith Rigby's work in the Montana Badlands.

Frontispiece: Keith Rigby, Jr., paleontologist, with young excavators.
Opposite: Sifting boxes used for screening out the smallest fossil fragments.

Printed in Singapore at Tien Wah Press.
1   2   3   4   5   6   7   8   9   10
Library of Congress Cataloging-in-Publication Data
Lasky, Kathryn.
Dinosaur dig/by Kathryn Lasky; photographs by Christopher G. Knight.
p.   cm.
Summary: Follows an East Coast family as it travels to Montana to
join a paleontology team in digging for dinosaur bones.
ISBN 0-688-08574-1—ISBN 0-688-08575-X (lib. bdg.)
1. Paleontology—Juvenile literature. 2. Dinosaurs—Juvenile
literature. [1. Paleontology. 2. Dinosaurs.] I. Knight,
Christopher G., ill. II. Title.
QE714.5.L36 1990
567.9' 1—dc20   89-13212   CIP   AC

qu-82

For Dawn Roetter — a patient listener

A Dream

Max Knight was imagining a world where dinosaurs once lived. If he squinted just so, those ivy-covered rocks of New England granite blurred and became the sandstone buttes of Montana, where, he had been told, the fossilized bones of dinosaurs now lay buried.

In a few days, Max and his sister, Meribah, and their parents would be leaving for the west to dig for dinosaur bones. They would be led in their search by Keith Rigby, Jr., a scientist from the University of Notre Dame. He is a special kind of scientist who studies the fossilized bones and remains of ancient life forms. These scientists are called *paleontologists*. Five other families would join the expedition to the Badlands of eastern Montana, the very country where five of the world's six *Tyrannosaurus rex* skeletons had been found.

◆　◆　◆

For weeks, Max had dreamed of finding teeth and horns and maybe even a flared collar of one of the armored dinosaurs. Meribah often fell asleep with a fistful of tiny plastic dinosaurs under her pillow. The whole family had seen movies about dinosaurs and read books about them, and now they were ready for the real thing.

Chris Knight, Max's father, had talked to Dr. Rigby on the phone to find out what they should take. There will be no running water, so the good news is that there will be no bathtubs or showers. The bad news is that the nearest ice cream cone is thirty-five miles away. Weather is hard to predict. Dr. Rigby said that it has been known to sleet as late as mid-June. During the day, it can get as hot as 110 degrees, and there can be winds of over a hundred miles per hour.

Kathryn, Max, and Meribah Knight at home in Cambridge.

They began to plan for these conditions. They made lists—lists of food, lists of gear, and lists of clothes. They checked their old camping equipment and decided that their tents were too old and the wrong shape to stand up to the wild winds of the Badlands. Chris ordered new tents of stronger materials, tents that were rounded, domed, so that the wind could wrap around them rather than blow them down.

◆ ◆ ◆

As the day of their departure drew near, Kathryn Knight, Max and Meribah's mother, felt herself being drawn back toward that time before time millions of years ago. One day she said, "Tomorrow we fly west, but, you know, I feel as if we'll be flying back—in time."

"Why? Aren't there buildings and highways and stores?" Meribah asked.

"Yes, but not nearly as many. The land is going to seem bigger and emptier, and we'll almost be able to imagine what it was like before there were any people there at all."

The gear piles up a few days before departure.

The Prairie

They spent their first night in a hotel in Billings, Montana. At five o'clock the next morning, they stuffed their two tents, four sleeping bags, four duffel bags of clothes, boxes of groceries, an ice chest, and a camp stove into the "rent-a-dent" station wagon they had picked up the night before at the car-rental agency. By 5:30, they were ready. They were leaving ceilings and walls, television, air conditioning, beds, and bathtubs behind. They were leaving time told by clocks for time measured by the sun. They were leaving for the Badlands.

◆　◆　◆

Before the Badlands, however, there is the grassland—the endless and undulating prairie. Once the grass was silvery green, but this is the second year of a long drought and the prairie looks scorched. By nine o'clock that morning, the temperature is 104 degrees and Max and Meribah have finished four juice boxes each and two cans of soda pop. The highway slides with shimmering mirages—pyramids, forests, whole cities spread before them. Actually, though, they pass only a few dusty little towns. As they drive, they begin to see great spools of tumbleweed caught against the barbed-wire cattle fences that go on for miles. The weed blows across the land until its freewheeling journey is interrupted by miles of fencing.

◆ ◆ ◆

At first, this was the land of the Sioux, the Crow, and the Assiniboine. When these Native Americans lost their struggle with the United States government, they were moved onto reservations, and the cattle barons came. They moved their huge herds of cattle along trails cut all the way from Texas, and they were masters of the land until the homesteaders arrived. Drought drove many of these farmers away. But before there were homesteaders or cattle barons or Sioux, before there were people, there were other living things, the ancient prehistoric animals that lived in this country for almost 200 million years.

This is an unimaginable number to Max and Meribah, so their parents try to make it imaginable. Chris explains that if the whole history of the earth were fitted into a calendar of one year, beginning on January first, dinosaurs would not have evolved until eleven months later, around December sixth.

"My birthday!" exclaims Max.

"They disappeared around Christmastime," his father adds.

"And people," Kathryn says, "would not have gotten here until sometime during the night of December thirty-first, and Columbus discovered America three seconds before midnight."

"So the dinosaurs were here for at least twenty days on this calendar, and we've only been here for a few minutes."

"You got it!" his dad says.

◆ ◆ ◆

The grass has grown thinner and the land has flattened out. Meribah spots her first cactus. Miles away, a plume of dark swirling air and sand moves across the barren land.

"Dust devils," Kathryn says, and opens a can of soda pop. They spot several closer to the highway, swirling up like poofs from genies' lamps.

A Montana highway cuts across the prairie.

Heading for the Badlands of northeastern Montana.

the shadows of scudding clouds. Black and startling, the hills spread across the dun-colored landscape. The shadows shift. They are no longer a dragon. They have become a crocodile slithering across the plains, its head pointing toward the north and west, its sculling tail tapering off toward the North Dakota border. The children whisper in the backseat.

"Imagine that this is a swamp," Max says in a low, dusty voice to his sister. "And this crocodile is watching the shoreline for prey."

Meribah's eyes open wide.

"Well, there was a swamp once," Max says. "Wasn't there, Mom?"

"It was more of a shallow sea," Kathryn replies.

"With crocodiles," Max says.

"With crocodiles," Kathryn repeats.

"And dinosaurs," Max adds.

"And dinosaurs, but that was at least sixty-five million years ago."

◆ ◆ ◆

The prairie has ended suddenly, and the landscape bare of grass and fences bursts into immense and rounded rock hills—the buttes. This is the beginning of the Badlands, so called because they are too barren and harsh for farming.

Then Chris slows the car suddenly. Miles ahead, it appears as if an immense dragon is crossing the road. The flat prairie has erupted into a range of sharply sculpted hills that is caught in

The prairie erupts into low, sculpted hills.

Slow Violence

The buttes herd against the sky like massive creatures grazing silently on an endless plain. Between the rocky hills, the land is cut and gouged.

Five hundred thousand years ago, much of North America was locked beneath a vast glacier. As the glacier began to loosen its icy grip and melt, it unleashed great torrents of water and ice that rushed in rivers southward from what is now Manitoba. These glacial runoffs jigsawed through this country, cutting the terrain into huge, jagged chunks. They left behind the buttes, the profiles of an even more ancient history.

In this area of Montana, the buttes are built from layers of different rock, sedimentary rocks that were deposited by seas, rivers, and glaciers. The layers are different colors: pale gray, gray-green, dark smoky brown, rosy pink, and light buff yellow. Some are made of river or channel sandstones, some come from mudstone shales and carbon-rich silts, some are pure carbon or coal layers, and one came from outer space. The rosy gray stripe is the iridium layer, and it was probably formed by the cosmic dust particles from an asteroid that hit the earth some 65 million years ago. Within these layers is a treasure trove of fossils.

A fossil is a trace of ancient life. It can be a footprint, a leaf print, a bone, or even impressions of skin. For fossilization to occur, however, certain things must happen. After an animal dies or a leaf from a plant falls, it must be covered quickly—before it begins to decay—by sand or mud. Then it must not be disturbed for a long, long time. The soft parts will eventually rot away, but the hard parts—the bones, the shell, the wood—will remain. Occasionally, soft parts, such as the skin of a dinosaur, do become fossilized. Over millions and millions of years, the mud or sand, rich in minerals, actually seeps into the bones or prints and turns these last remains to stone, preserving them forever.

The buttes of Montana—graveyard of the dinosaurs.

*The buttes, stone sandwiches of
sandstone, silt, shale, and coal.*

The part of the story that the Knights have come to learn about is set in the Mesozoic Era, which is sometimes called the age of reptiles. The Mesozoic Era began around 225 million years ago and lasted for about 160 million years. This is when the dinosaurs lived. The last period of the Mesozoic, from 136 to 65 million years ago, is called the Cretaceous. During the Cretaceous Period, there was the greatest variety of dinosaurs. At the end of this period, the dinosaurs began to decline and then mysteriously disappeared from the earth forever.

The buttes have stilled time. Within their layers of sandstone, shale, silt, and coal, they hold a story that has been waiting to be read since the dinosaurs disappeared 65 million years ago. Erosion lets the story be told. Erosion is the wearing away of the earth by weather—wind, rain and flooding, and all of the natural forces that shape the earth. It is through erosion that fossils long covered are exposed. They literally "weather out" from the earth. Erosion, in a sense, is the process by which the book is opened and the pages of the story are turned for reading.

The ancient shallow sea of the dinosaurs' world vanished. The land was split by a new sea, and oceans rose and fell. To the west, the Rocky Mountains thrust from the plains; the glaciers came and went. With this slow violence, the skin of the earth was gradually pulled back, leaving the land of the dead bones to rise with the buttes that soar one thousand feet into the Montana sky.

The Camp in the Emptiness

Two of Max and Meribah's good friends, Sam and Emily Handlin, and their parents have also come to Montana to dig for dinosaur bones. The families meet sixty miles from Glasgow, Montana, on a high bluff overlooking an immense reservoir. Here they will make their camp. It is smack in the middle of the dinosaur country. Max and Meribah and their friends stand on the edge of the bluff and stare back at the Badlands.

"It's so empty," Meribah whispers to no one.

The families camp on a bluff above the Fort Peck Reservoir.

Just as eyes grow accustomed to the dark and are able to pick out the shapes and features of the night, the children's eyes grow accustomed to the emptiness, and they begin to see the things that live and somehow grow in this wild, harsh country. Their eyes alert, they find the life of the Badlands—the delicate sego lilies, like white stars scattered through the thin grass, the bluebells, the spikes of yuccas, and, growing close to the ground, the prickly pear cactus with its pale blossoms the colors of ice cream. There is the sudden white flash of an antelope's tail, and in the lengthening shadow of a nearby butte, a mule deer stands twitching its ears. There is a flicker of black and white in the grass nearby as magpies dart into flight. There are meadowlarks, too, and even bluebirds. Everywhere, there is the sweet, pungent scent of the sagebrush. The children watch it all.

A stiff wind moves across the silvery grass of the bluff's topland. It turns the grass dark and ripples through it like a current. Suddenly, it seems as if there are rivers of wind coursing through the grass.

Max walks to the edge of the bluff and squints his eyes, trying to envision the still waters of a dark lagoon as *Anatosaurus*, a duckbill dinosaur, peers from the water. There was no grass back then, only low shrubs we call *sedges*. Gigantic palms, vines, and plants with huge fronds grew along the banks and on the islands and in the marsh-lands of this sea, and new upstart flowering plants were beginning to replace the evergreens and firs.

The sea swept inland from what is now the Gulf of Mexico and spread north to the Arctic and west to where the Rocky Mountains would eventually rise. It is difficult to imagine that a sea ever existed in this vast land that is now made up of hot, blue sky, parched earth, wind, and silence.

◆　◆　◆

The bluff looks down on the Fort Peck Reservoir, completed in 1940, one of the largest reservoirs in the world. A pale moon hangs in the thin gray sky and the night is still. But about 4:30 in the morning, the wind begins to blow, and in just five minutes, the air is snapping with the lashing and flapping of tent flies.

Spikes of yucca growing in a harsh land.

"Reports of turbulence ahead." The merry voices come from Max and Sam's tent. They sound as excited as if they were on a wild ride at an amusement park. The tent in which Kathryn, Chris, and Meribah are sleeping seems ready to buck and fly with the wind.

◆　◆　◆

Chris jumps up and is outside in a flash. Above the howl of the wind, he yells to the children to get their tents down, and then to David Handlin, Sam's father:

"We've got to move the cars closer and make a windbreak to protect these tents."

Kathryn tries to reassure Meribah that this is "just a little windstorm, dear." But Max shouts, "Little? Are you crazy, Mom?" His dust-covered face peers through the opening of their tent. "Watch this." He steps a few feet away from the tent, out of the lee of the car, and flings himself, howling with laughter, upon the wind. Balanced only on the tips of his toes and spread-eagled against the wind, which supports him entirely, he looks as if he is about to fly.

They try to have breakfast, but the cereal blows out of the bowls and the milk flies from the carton like spume off the crest of a wave.

◆　◆　◆

Three hours later, the storm blows itself out. There is sand in everything, from the cuffs of their pants to the seams of a book. Their eyes are bleary and red from the storm, their hair gritty. At eight o'clock that morning, Keith Rigby drives up in his pickup.

Keith Rigby, left, talks dinosaurs with geologist Robert Sloan.

"Welcome to Montana!" He is a very large man, as is his friend and colleague Robert Sloan from the University of Minnesota, who has just driven up also. The two men have not seen each other in some time and almost immediately pull out a few small fossil pieces from their pockets to compare. There are several jokes about the windstorm.

"That's why we have come here. The wind, the best excavator, does your work for you, never gets tired, never complains," Keith says.

Robert Sloan looks out over the broken terrain toward the buttes. "It just keeps getting better and better out here," he says, meaning that the wind and the other forces of erosion keep revealing more evidence of the dinosaurs every year.

The children are already bombarding both men with questions. They have found several small bones. "Are these dinosaur bones?"

"No," Keith answers patiently. "I think someone had barbecued ribs out here. They look like pig bones to me."

"What about this?" Emily holds up a smooth, rusty-looking knob.

"That is a concretion!" He says the word slowly.

"A concretion!" Emily's face lights up. "What's that?"

"A rock, a fancy name for a rock."

"Oh." Emily's face crumbles.

"Don't worry," Keith assures her. "You're going to find plenty of bones."

"Where?" Meribah asks.

"Today at the Bug Creek Anthills," Keith replies. "The other families in our group are joining us here and then we're off."

The Bug Creek Anthills

Children and their parents climb into the back of two pickup trucks. Keith closes the tailgates. "We're heading for the richest fossil site of the entire Mesozoic!" he announces.

In 1906, local homesteaders gathered along a dried-out creekbed to observe an odd sight. Stretched out for nearly one hundred feet were the bones of what appeared to be the skeleton of a gigantic insect. A group of men hovered around the bones. One of them was wearing a bowler-type hat, gold-rimmed pince-nez glasses, and shiny boots that seemed to defy the dust and grit of the terrain. The well-dressed man was the famous paleontologist and dinosaur hunter Barnum Brown. He and his crew had just completed the first excavation of the world's largest carnivore, *Tyrannosaurus rex*. The homesteaders had never heard the word *dinosaur*, let alone *Tyrannosaurus rex*.

"Mighty big bug you got there!" one of them said. The name stuck, and since then the site, laden with anthills, has been known as the Bug Creek Anthills.

There are anthills still, scores of them. Although most paleontologists came to look for "the big guys"—*Tyrannosaurus* and *Triceratops*—some,like Robert Sloan and Keith Rigby, were interested in smaller fare, those small mammals that overlapped in time with the dinosaurs toward the end of the Cretaceous.

In 1963, when Robert Sloan first visited the Anthills, he wasn't expecting much. He wasn't interested in dinosaur bones, but he'd heard rumors that fossil evidence of early mammals had been spotted there, too. His companion, who was driving, told him to make it quick, as he had a party to get to in Glasgow, which was sixty-five miles away.

Within five minutes, Bob Sloan had filled a pillbox with tiny teeth belonging to a dozen different kinds of early mammals. Over the next twenty years he and his associate Leigh Van Valen would find evidence of eighteen more, thus doubling our knowledge of the small mammals who lived near the end of the Cretaceous. Bob began to suspect

Heading for the Bug Creek Anthills.

that the Bug Creek Anthills had a story to tell, of a time when the dinosaurs were dying, species by species, and mammals were coming into their own. It was the mammals' fossilized teeth and bone slivers that the ants of the region used to fortify their anthills against the terrible winds.

After bouncing over nearly invisible dirt roads, the trucks have arrived at what appears to be a big cone-shaped hole in the earth. It is a quarry that Keith Rigby and Bob Sloan have been excavating over the last two decades, sifting through tons of dirt in their efforts to draw a picture of life at what is called the KT boundary, that borderline time between the Cretaceous and the Tertiary Period that followed.

The group will be digging in a formation of rock called the Hell Creek Formation. A formation of rock is a layer of traceable strata that can run for miles and has certain identifiable characteristics that tell its age and composition and make it distinguishable from other rock. The Hell Creek Formation is made of gray-green sandstone rock from the late Cretaceous.

Near the top of the Hell Creek Formation is the rose-gray streak that signals iridium—evidence, most likely, that an asteroid struck the earth with tremendous force. Some people believe that the dinosaurs met a sudden and violent end when the asteroid struck, but Keith Rigby and Robert Sloan feel otherwise. They believe that the dinosaurs died out gradually, for many reasons, and that by the time the iridium layer was laid down, many kinds were extinct already. But some went on, overlapping for as long as 500,000 years with the early mammals that would eventually replace them. They are seeking to prove their theory in the sediments of the Bug Creek Anthills, later in time than the iridium layer when all dinosaurs are said to have died.

Bob Sloan drives up in his truck with his students from the University of Minnesota just as Keith arrives. Bob and his students will be working a dozen yards away on the next hillock. Keith's first instructions to his group are simple.

"Get ready to sniff dirt, folks!"

"What do you mean by that?" Emily asks Keith.

"I want your noses this far off the ground." Keith smiles as he raises his hand to his nose.

Dr. Rigby demonstrates how to "sniff dirt."

A tall thirteen-year-old girl holds out her hand to show Keith what she has found.

"Ah ha, now Jennifer here, she's got a piece of salamander skull. See, it's pitted on top there and rough, kind of grainy on the other side. Max, you've got an *Edmontosaurus* tooth—a fragment of one—and a garfish vertebra," he says, picking up a dense, cylindrical piece about one half an inch long. "You see," he says, pointing to one end, "this end is rounded, and the other is concave. You can imagine how they might fit together into a column for a backbone. And I think you've got a piece of an ancient turtle shell."

There are so many signs of ancient life that

To sniff dirt, they must get down on hands and knees and crawl over the sandy terrain with their noses inches from the ground.

"Is this a bone?"

"No, that's a rock," says Keith. "Look at its even texture and color."

A handful of small fossil fragments.

they can almost imagine themselves in a gigantic aquarium gone to desert.

Max goes back to the place where he found the tooth and crawls to the base of a cliff with a large overhanging edge. Pressed within the shadow of the cliff, he starts to explore its wall.

The children and their parents learn fast. Within a short time, they can tell the difference between a bone and a rock—and the treasures keep coming. "I call that a croco-gator," Keith says, handing back a small, platelike piece that is the scute or scale of either an alligator or a crocodile.

Above: Max scrapes at a sandstone wall.
Right: Dr. Rigby identifies a fossil fragment from an ancient "croco-gator."

There are hundreds of garfish scales. Garfish, among the most ancient of fish, still exist. They swam throughout the old Cretaceous lakes and rivers and their scales are scattered everywhere in the Anthills. The scales are shiny and dark, except for those that have a blue tinge. They may have turned blue from having been digested by a crocodile. There are also mouse-sized jaws and teeth from the early mammals. The children's and their parents' plastic bags are filling up.

"Who would like to see a living neighborhood resident?" Bob Sloan has walked over from the area where his students are digging. Cupped in the palm of his hand is a small, pale-green horned toad. Bob is stroking its belly to put it to sleep so it will not be frightened as the people crowd around to look at it more closely.

"Looks like an ankylosaur, doesn't it?" Bob whispers. "They use these fellows for imitation dinosaurs in horror films." The small toad is now sleeping peacefully in his hand. Bob sets it down. The green color drains from the toad as it turns tan and indistinguishable in color from the sandstone slab on which it now awakens.

A living resident of the Bug Creek Anthills.

"Time for the shovels!" Keith announces. He gives a brief demonstration of how to fill a burlap bag.

"A bag of dirt," Keith says, "can tell us more about the web of life in this region than can one single dinosaur bone. We can find out what else lived here, what grew here, what animals ate, and what ate them. And it's faster than crawling around sniffing dirt."

"Then why did we do it?" someone asks.

"Because by crawling and sniffing, you learn what to look for."

Max and Sam work together in the shadow of the hanging cliff. They fill bag after bag with dirt.

Only a ton of dirt to go!

"Don't make the bags too heavy, folks," Keith cautions as he watches Meribah and Emily stagger with a bag to load onto a truck.

By the end of the morning, just about the time the temperature hits 106 degrees, the children and their parents have bagged over a ton of dirt. They climb into the trucks to go back to the reservoir.

Emily and Meribah haul a burlap bag to a waiting truck.

My Father's Eyes

Keith settles in behind the wheel of a pickup truck and takes a long drink from his canteen. The brim of his cowboy hat casts a slashing shadow across his face. He begins to tell how he came to hunt dinosaur bones.

"I became a geological field assistant at the ripe age of three."

Keith's father, Keith Rigby, Sr., is one of the world's foremost experts on fossil sponges. He was working back then in a geological formation in western Texas called the Texas Reef Complex. Three-year-old Keith would climb into his dad's old combat backpack, and together they would strike out across the barren flats looking for fossils.

"I learned pretty quickly what to pick up. You see, my dad was legally blind, so I became my father's eyes."

Eventually, many years after he outgrew the combat backpack, he went to Brigham Young University, where he earned his bachelor's degree in geology. After Brigham Young, he went on to Columbia University, where he earned master's and doctor's degrees in the study of vertebrate paleontology. Vertebrates are animals with backbones, and that is what Keith studied—ancient life forms that had backbones, or spines.

As they drive, Keith stops to point out landmarks and sites and geological features. He doesn't find it hard to imagine what the land looked like 65 million years ago. "This was the edge of the Cretaceous sea. There were streams and river channels, and that's where we find most of the bones—in the river and channel stones of the buttes. Things back then would have been flatter, like a savannah—a treeless plain—but with no grasses. These little sego lilies"—he waves toward the tiny starlike flowers that blow in the light breeze—"they showed up about thirty million years ago. When the dinosaurs

Dr. Rigby scans the buttes.

lived, there were palms, reeds, and cypress. There were probably some shorebirds. It was open and not jungly, like in the movies. I figure the dinosaurs must have traveled in herds. In the jungle, you can't have herds. Can't see the other fellow."

"Why did the dinosaurs die?" Kathryn asks.

"Who knows? MTV?" He winks. "There've been more stupid theories about dinosaur extinction than you can believe. Some people say they had a death wish or that they were poisoned by the new flowers that were evolving! Fallen arches, yes, that's one. Constant gravity caused them to collapse from their own weight!"

"What about the asteroid?"

"Not a bad idea. But the fact is the dinosaurs stuck around for up to several hundred thousand years after it hit. We're finding that out right here. So it wasn't the asteroid alone. It could have been a combination of things. The climate had been cooling for maybe fifty million years, the seas fell, and those new furry little creatures, whose bones are all over the Bug Creek Anthills, were beginning to multiply and get a foothold." He pauses. "No easy answers," he says quietly, although he does not seem in the least disturbed by this.

106 Degrees and Rising

"Yeeow!" Kathryn yelps as she sprints barefoot across the low sandstone slabs. The slabs are as hot as a griddle, and her feet are scorched. She races toward the cool wet sands on the banks of the reservoir and sets down an empty box with a screen at the bottom. The others are standing knee-deep in the cool water of the reservoir, gently sloshing the boxes back and forth. They are filled with the contents from the burlap bags.

Cool work— sloshing sifting boxes on the banks of the Fort Peck Reservoir.

Sam and Max slosh and sift, hoping to find fossil treasures.

The dirt, the sand, any particle smaller than the very, very tiny openings of the screen will wash out. Dry grass and bits of twigs or sagebrush will then be floated off by carefully sinking the screen until it fills. The floating bits will drift away. What is left in the bottom of the screen is "the payload."

"Now I want you all to stop for a moment," Keith says, wading into the water. The sloshing stops as children and adults turn toward Keith. He raises his arms. "Aaarghhh!" There is a splash.

"Hang on to your boxes!" someone shouts. "Surf's up!"

Keith Rigby has just belly flopped into the reservoir, clothes and all.

He surfaces and rolls over on his back, as playful and as graceful as one of the larger aquatic mammals. People begin following him. "It's wetter swimming with clothes," Max says.

It *is* a funny feeling to swim with the clinging wet clothes. They fill with pockets of air and then deflate and tug gently at the body, creating swirls and eddies as one swims. Everyone forgets the boxes and floats and drifts on the placid waters of the reservoir, looking up at the cloudless sky.

Taking a welcome plunge.

This excavator sorts through the payload.

The temperature is 106 degrees and still rising. For the rest of the afternoon, the children and their parents will sift, slosh, and swim.

By that evening, one part of the story about the very end of the Cretaceous will seem a little more complete. The prehistoric community of the Bug Creek Anthills will be revealed, in part, by the tiny bone fragments left behind. It was a teeming place filled with at least twelve species of dinosaurs, Keith's croco-gators, salamanders, hoofed creatures the size of dogs, and early mam-

mals, no bigger than the smallest mice. They all left fossil traces behind, and a tiny number of these have been caught in the fine mesh of the screen boxes. From a ton of matrix—the dirt and sand excavated by the children and their parents—seventy dinosaur teeth and one thousand teeth from mammals, lizards, frogs, and crocodiles will eventually be "screened." And there will be fragments of vertebrae and every kind of bone from dozens of other species of animals, as well. After the bones are collected and sorted, they will be sent to Keith's laboratory at Notre Dame for further study. No bones will be taken home. It's against the law to collect bones on public lands for private collections, unless you have a permit from the government.

An Edmontosaurus *tooth and fragment.*

Big Bones

It is the second day of the dinosaur dig. The group is taking two trucks. Keith will drive one truck and Chris Knight will drive the second.

"Ready for some adventures, sports fans?" Keith asks, and waggles his eyebrows up and down as the children crowd into his truck. He slams the tailgate shut.

Ten minutes later, they turn off the highway onto a dusty imprint of a road. The ride gets bouncy and the children squeal. The imprint of the road grows dimmer. The ride gets rougher and begins to make a roller coaster seem tame and predictable by comparison. Within three minutes, any sign of a road has vanished. Keith stops the truck and gets out.

"There's a road here somewhere," he calls to Chris. He climbs back inside and looks out through the windshield. "Ah ha!" he says suddenly. "See that butte over there?" He points through the windshield. "That's where we want to get to."

It seems impossible. The country is cut up like a three-dimensional jigsaw puzzle. There are canyons between here and the butte, chasms and parched and rutted land with cracks big enough to swallow a truck wheel. The trucks bounce on over sagebrush, prickly pear, and rock.

"Hold on, folks!" The trucks plunge over the lip of a wash, a kind of sunken beach of flat gray sand where a river once flowed but has long since dried up. For a quarter of a mile, they follow this river's ghost.

A rough ride in the Badlands.

"How do we get out of here?" Keith grumbles. It seems as if they've sunk into a hole with jagged edges. The sides of the wash rise steeply. The earth is shaley and crumbly, but Keith starts the engine and heads directly toward the wall of the wash. He shifts into a lower gear.

"Hang on, sports fans!" he yells, and guns the truck on up the side of the wash. Chris follows.

The trucks with their cargo of laughing children and half-stunned adults are out and jiggling across a grassy topland. Keith plunges down the side of an arroyo, a dry gulch. As they come up the other side, a herd of antelope strings out against the sky as if in a race with the clouds. The trucks roar on, and then Keith slams on the brakes. They've stopped just where the land drops away—at the rim of the world.

Below are the domes of buttes. They are like immense dark bubbles boiling up against the clear blue sky. Their striped sediments rise in bands of color.

"We are not looking for tiny slivers today," Keith announces.

"Do you think we'll find some big bones?" Max asks.

"Possibly. Look sharp. Look for washouts where you might see scatterings of smaller bone fragments already eroded out. The bones come in all colors—dark brown, reddish, gray. Then you look for a piece just weathering out. You can scrape with this." He holds up a sharp, pointed tool called an *awl*. "But first, some words of caution. Be careful with your awl. Keep it in your backpack until you need it. Second, keep drinking a lot of water from your canteen. If you start to feel weird, pour water right onto your head. If you notice your neighbor is turning bright red, pour some water on his or her head. We don't want any sunstroke. Keep your hat on. Finally, there are rattlesnakes out here. If you drop something down a hole, don't reach in. If you think you're going to fall and start to grab for a root or some sagebrush, make sure it is just that. While you hike, keep talking so they'll know you're coming and you won't surprise them." He pauses. "Okay, troops, let's go."

On the rim of the world!

The Elephant's Hide

As the crow flies, it is perhaps two hundred yards to the next butte. To reach that point, however, it is necessary to go down three hundred feet into the boiling cauldron of domed buttes, thread through the broken land, and then climb up the other side. They begin their descent on a sheer face of earth. It is the side of one of the domes, sheathed in dark gray siltstone that has swelled and folded into deep wrinkles that look exactly like the hide of an elephant's back.

Meribah and her mother are among the last of the group to descend. At first, the downward climb is not difficult, but then it gets steeper and the siltstone slides out from under their feet in little avalanches. They go slower, holding each other's hands for balance. By the time they make it down, they can see the others, but they are far behind them.

"Well, we're off the elephant's back," Meribah announces, and skips ahead of her mother. She is following a dry creekbed that is twisting between the buttes.

"Wait up!" her mother calls. They must find the trail that leads up the far side of the cauldron.

♦ ♦ ♦

They begin to climb along the high embankment of the creek, moving like inchworms. It takes them a full three minutes to go one foot.

They are both scared. There seems to be no such thing as a foothold. The way has become steeper. Beneath their sturdy shoes, the earth starts to slide. The cocoa-colored marbles of siltstone roll and crumble, and the sides of the embankment begin to slide away. They are high up. There are no handholds except for the sagebrush and clumps of wire grass and the occasional root.

Above: Kathryn and Meribah on the elephant's hide.
Left: Traversing the boiling cauldron.

Every twig has the potential of coiling into hissing life, a rattlesnake set to strike. Meribah and her mother have become part of the eroding strata of rock and earth.

The other people are clearly visible on top of a ridge. Yet, for all practical purposes, they have receded entirely from the world where Kathryn and her daughter, Meribah, are climbing. Their voices are only dim scratches in the wind.

"Do you know your way? Mommy?" Tracks of tears run down Meribah's dusty cheeks.

"I think so," Kathryn answers. "Let's remember to talk to keep the rattlesnakes away." It is hard to talk when you are scared, and they soon run out of words, so they begin to chant nursery rhymes.

"The snakes must know we're coming," Meribah says. She has just started to shout "Peter, Peter, Pumpkin-Eater" at the sky when her feet begin to slide again. Her mother's begin to slide, too. They curl their toes in their boots and grab at the elephant's hide. The siltstone has turned gray and wrinkly once more.

Finally, they reach the ridge where the others are waiting. Down they climb again. When they hit bottom, they realize, by the color of the sediments, that they've dropped into the Cretaceous. Keith Rigby gestures toward a sloping incline.

The treacherous descent.

A brave girl finally cries.

They follow a ribbon of dark gray sediment, and with each step up, they pass through fifty thousand years of time until, once again, they enter the Hell Creek Formation.

This time, Meribah and her mother are careful to stay very close to the others. The way is easy now, and there is time to stop and scrape with the awls, looking for the big bones that might be weathering out. Within five minutes, Emily and her mother have actually stumbled across something.

"Keith! Keith!" they both call.

"What'cha got?" He crawls up the slope where they are. "Ah ha!" he exclaims. The two syllables ring out like a bell pealing the news that this must be a dinosaur find.

The fossil has completely weathered out. In color, it is a deep chocolate brown. It is the size of a heavy-duty block and tackle weighing at least four pounds—the kind used to move grand pianos out of third-story windows. However, this block did not help to move a piano. It is a vertebra and was part of the backbone of a dinosaur.

A dinosaur vertebra weighing about four pounds.

"Ceratopsian," Keith says, meaning that it belonged to one of the horn-faced dinosaurs like *Triceratops*. He turns it over with both of his hands. "Let's see if there is any more of this fellow around."

The children and their parents scrape and dig for another twenty minutes but find nothing. Other fossil hunters may have excavated the rest of the creature, or this single piece may have been moved by water, erosion, or an ancient predator far from where the animal's body once lay.

The group moves on. Fifteen minutes later, they reach a saddle between two buttes that has been scooped out by wind and erosion. One of the children says, "What's that?" There is a curve of red bowing out of the earth. Keith is standing nearby. "Oh ho ho!" He drops to his knees and begins scraping away the earth. "This is a rib, the part that attaches to the vertebra." He only scrapes for three or four minutes, revealing a nubbin at the end of the rib's curve.

Keith sits back on his heels and looks around. He casually picks up a handful of surface rocks. From this handful, he picks. up a small straight piece slightly larger than a matchstick. "Ossified tendon." Tendon is the stringlike tissue that attaches muscle to bone. He holds up the piece so everyone can see it and then passes it around.

"They're all over the place." Soon the group is finding hundreds of the matchstick pieces with their straight, grained surfaces. Keith Rigby looks a few feet down from where the original bone was found. "There're all sorts of scraps down there." These are good signs, signs that there might be more than a single bone, possibly the remains of a whole creature that still lies buried in these sediments.

"Okay, guys! Get your picks, get your trowels."

Above: A fossilized rib juts out of the earth. Right: Scraping away with awls at the earth surrounding the fossil.

They are digging in the heart of the Hell Creek Formation, in what was mud that edged an ancient stream or river. Keith knows the dates of these particular sediments to within a gnat's eyelash. They are 67 to 68 million years old.

After fifteen minutes of scraping with trowels and picks, they expose two beautiful feet of rib, as well as a good portion of vertebrae.

"What kind of dinosaur?"

"Don't know yet," Keith mutters.

He is asked this question at least five times in the next forty-five minutes, and each time he replies very softly and patiently, "Don't know." It is as if the softer his voice becomes, the more excitement he is trying to muffle. He pauses and looks up.

"So, sports fans"—he points with his trowel—"we need to peel that stuff back over there." He means the ground, the earth, the river sediments. "We've got another rib coming up, and it's going thataway." He points with his trowel to the west. "So off with the hill!" Eighteen inches later, this second rib is still going. The first rib is now revealed to a length of three feet. Two more rib heads that attach the ribs to the vertebrae are uncovered.

"Keep away from the bone with your picks," Keith instructs. He pauses. "This vertebra inter-

A vertebra begins to emerge.

ests me. This could be, and this is only a very rough field call . . . barely a hunch . . . " He stops, starts, and lurches forward as if he is stepping around his next words. "Well, this could be an ankylosaur." *Ankylosaurus* was a plant-eating, armored dinosaur around seventeen feet long. Keith bases his hunch on the transverse processes—the pieces of bone that project out of the side of the vertebrae. "They have a very peculiar structure," he says. "They seem short and thick."

Armored dinosaurs such as *Ankylosaurus* had stout processes, thick and very dense to support the armor.

"It's very foolish to even hope, though," Keith adds quickly. "There are only two really complete ankylosaurs that have ever been found."

The group, however, does not think it is foolish at all, and they work even harder.

Two hours, five ribs, and three vertebrae later, Keith is still unwilling to make a firm field call on what type of dinosaur this is. His hopes for an *Ankylosaurus* are fading. He is not sure what they have uncovered, but the excavation is becoming more complicated than he had anticipated, especially with an inexperienced crew. He is too excited to call it off, however. Tomorrow they will have to come back with the proper materials to continue the excavation.

A piece of rib sails out of the earth.

◆ ◆ ◆

For now, they all stand back and look at the bones. They grow suddenly quiet, each person absorbed in thought. Kathryn, for one, is stunned by the realization that this is the first sunlight that has touched these bones, buried for 67 million years, and that the small group of people standing on this saddleback are the first humans ever to see these bones. She has made a connection with a time she barely believed existed. She bends down to touch a rib. It is smooth and red. She is thrilled by the very touch, this touch of life even in death.

◆ ◆ ◆

In the pink-gray twilight, they sit outside their tents. Too tired to cook anything fancy, they roast hot dogs and drink soda pop and look at the sky, seeing dinosaurs in the clouds. One cloud resembling a shark is actually a thunderhead punching across the Montana sky; but the rain never comes. Twilight drains into dusk, and the long blue dusk dissolves into night.

Dinosaur ribs over four feet in length.

The Endless Story

They are up shortly after dawn the next morning. By eight o'clock, they have transported their materials for a full excavation to the site: the household cement, paintbrushes, trowels, picks, awls, burlap bags, a twenty-five-pound bag of plaster of paris, and fifty-pound containers of water, as well as mixing tubs and resin hardeners. They have lugged all of this across the elephant's hide, through the countless gullies, coulees—the gulches gouged out by rainstorms—and the dry creeks, over the ridge and to the saddleback where the ancient bones have lain hidden.

The crew divides up. Some continue excavating. Others, with tin snips, cut the burlap bags into strips four inches wide by two feet long. The bones now sail out of the earth like an old Viking ship.

The excavating has become more delicate. They must be careful with their awls as they undercut the bones. The object is to clear out as much of the earth as gently as possible from under the bones and to leave small pedestals for support.

Left: Hiking into the site with additional excavation materials.
Right: Scraping carefully with awls and trowels.

Little chunks of bone are bound to break off. Keith takes the household cement and glues these small parts of the fossil puzzle back into place. After gluing in the top part of the rib that attaches to the main part, or centrum, of the vertebra, he calls for his paintbrush and whisks off the dust. Staring at it, he begins to speak slowly. "You know, this is a long rib, well over three feet. This is no ankylosaur. *Ankylosaurus* has very bowed ribs. More cow than deer," he says, referring to its shape.

As more bones are excavated into the sunlight, the entire fossil construction seems to become more fragile and complex. People's voices soften and drop. They move their tools more delicately, beginning to sense where the weak spots are. They gasp when the tapering end of one rib seems on the brink of crumbling away. It is time for the hardeners.

A youngster is sent to fetch the Glyptal from a backpack. Glyptal is a resin used for sealing electrical connections, but it works nicely as a hardener for fragile fossil bones. Keith pours it on the bone liberally, letting it soak in and dry.

Left: The work becomes even more delicate as the fossil is exposed.
Right: Pouring on resin to harden the fossil.

He touches up the places that he missed with a small paintbrush. A few minutes later, he will give it a second coat. After this second coat, he wraps the hardened bone in clear plastic wrap. Then he directs the plaster mixers to get to work. The twenty-five-pound bag of plaster of paris is lugged, along with a fifty-pound water jug, over to a dishpan. Keith takes a swig before pouring water into the dishpan over the dry plaster powder.

"Mix it up good and smooth. No lumps, please."

Max and Meribah and their friends plunge their hands into the thick, white, cool mixture.

"Goosh it! Squoosh it!" Meribah chants under her breath.

"It feels like mud." "No, frosting!" they exclaim. It is a wonderful feeling, a new texture in this country of hot, dry earth and crumbling rock.

When the plaster is ready, they must work quickly. The people who cut the burlap strips pass them to the plasterers, who dip them in the wet plaster and then hand them to Keith, who drapes them onto the bone over the plastic wrap and then molds them as closely and as carefully as he can to the shape of the bone.

Mixing up plaster of paris (left) and cutting strips of burlap (right) to make casts for the fossil bones.

In the meantime, other people are still cutting away under the bone to bring it into higher relief from the ground so that the plaster strips can encase it as completely as possible. Others work along the bone just ahead of Keith in order to patch in any small pieces that have dropped out. Any pieces that cannot be patched in are numbered with a pen and put into a plastic bag. The work is intense and hot. Keith, however, reminds

Above: Hardened with resin, a fossil is covered in plastic wrap.
Left: A strip of burlap is dipped in plaster of paris.
Opposite: Preparing to fortify the bone in a cast of burlap and plaster.

Wrapping the bones with the wet plaster strips.

people to keep drinking water as the sun rides high in the sky. "Don't worry about running out of water. I'd rather have the water go into you than into the plaster of paris."

"I feel like a statue," Meribah whispers when the plaster on her hands and face begins to dry in the hot, dry air.

As the plastering is progressing, another rib is

Covered with plaster in Montana!

discovered. People are racing now to splint the longest rib of the six excavated so far, as it appears quite fragile. A piece of twisted sagebrush is measured against the bone for a splint.

"Every bone is a challenge. It's like pick-up sticks," Keith says, sitting back for a minute. He is looking at the trucks on the ridge one-half mile away. They will have to transport all of these bones across the broken country to the trucks. When completely plastered, the bones will weigh several hundred pounds. As yet, they have found no trace of a head, but Keith thinks he knows what the head would look like if it was found. It would have three horns and a deep frill of neck armor sweeping back. "It's a *Triceratops*," he says shortly before noon. "That's a field call, mind you." Back in his laboratory at Notre Dame in the fall, he will confirm it.

"But where's the head?" Max asks.

"Maybe in a museum someplace."

The previous day, shortly before they left the site, Keith discovered some old chunks of plaster, a sign that someone else had been excavating in this site perhaps as long as seventy to eighty years ago. Back in the early part of this century, perhaps only the head had begun to weather out, leaving the rest of the creature buried, or too inaccessible to excavate. In any case, he was sure that the head was not here.

Fossils encased in the protective plaster cast.

The plaster on the bones has dried. In their casts, the bones are now ready to be lifted from their 67-million-year-old grave. Along one four-and-one-half-foot rib, people line up crouched on their knees. They work their hands underneath the bone and supporting earth to where it has been cut away. With his awl, Keith will pick out the pedestals at the last minute. And then: "One . . . two . . . three . . . flip!" he calls. The earth yields. The bone is turned.

Teamwork is essential in protecting the ancient bones.

They work even faster now, with more hardener, more plastic wrap, and more plaster to encase and protect the underneath side. By early afternoon, the sky glares down, cloudless, pressing on them like hot sheet metal. The temperature is nearing 110 degrees. Some of the people are looking dangerously flushed. Keith wants to move them out quickly. It will be too hard to take all the bones out today. He plans to come back again for the rest. He instructs everyone to take a big drink of water. Then the larger bones are shouldered by the grown-ups. The children stagger under loads of water jugs and backpacks filled with tools. In a short time, they have learned how to maneuver across the rough country. Even on the steepest slope, the one leading up to the ridge where the trucks are, they manage to claw their way to the top without dropping a pack or a water jug. The bones are safely on their way to Keith's laboratory for study.

◆ ◆ ◆

The *Triceratops* bones have been brought down the butte toward the close of their last day in the Badlands. It is near the time of Midsummer Night, when the sun sets late and the campfire is needed more for warmth than for light. Max and Meribah and their parents listen to Keith Rigby's stories until it is too late to do anything but go to bed. In this short night between two long days, they watch through their tent windows as the moon rises and sails over the ancient buttes, over the rattlesnakes and the bones, over the antelope and the coyote, over the stories locked in the sandstone. The real black of the night is a long time coming. It seeps in slowly at first, and then, finally, the darkness flows all around the sleeping people. Toward dawn, a timeless wind will rise and blow through the grass and wrap around the buttes and scrape away at those stories. It takes only a year or two or three for a bone that has weathered out to be destroyed by the same forces that have uncovered it.

Bringing the bones out of the Badlands.

Time reveals the stories of the immense and powerful dinosaurs and of the tiny mammals who replaced them. However, it would all be lost without paleontologists such as Keith Rigby who watch patiently and crawl over the ancient terrains, sniffing dirt, scraping away at the earth with their awls and trowels, and always wondering what could have lived there and how.

◆ ◆ ◆

Kathryn looks at Meribah asleep in her sleeping bag. She remembers their scary time on the elephant's hide, but the fear melts away in the darkness of the night. In the tent next door, she hears Max stir. She watches the blackness, and through it she can see the form of a butte like the hump of a lizard's back rising against the night sky. The stars come out and the constellations begin to stitch their lacy designs across the darkness. A stillness swallows the land, and the starry bear climbs over the lizard's spine while the rest of the story waits to be heard.